Farm Fresh Fun

Farm Fresh Fun

VEERA HIRANANDANI

illustrated by CHRISTINE ALMEDA

PENGUIN WORKSHOP

PENGUIN WORKSHOP
An Imprint of Penguin Random House LLC, New York

 First published in 2014 by Grosset & Dunlap. This edition published in 2020 by Penguin Workshop, an imprint of Penguin Random House LLC, New York. PENGUIN and PENGUIN WORKSHOP are trademarks of Penguin Books Ltd, and the W colophon is a registered trademark of Penguin Random House LLC. Printed in the USA.

Visit us online at www.penguinrandomhouse.com.

Library of Congress Control Number: 2014030493

ISBN 9780593096918 (paperback) 10 9 8 7 6 5 4 3 2 1
ISBN 9780593096925 (library binding) 10 9 8 7 6 5 4 3 2 1

For **David, Hannah, and Eli,**
my best readers and eaters
—VH

For **Vanessa and Wolfie**
—CA

Chapter One

Guess what? A very exciting and lucky thing is about to happen to me! This Monday, our class is going on a field trip to Goat Hill Farm. At first I thought they only had goats there. But Mrs. B, my third-grade teacher, says they also have apples (that we get to pick off the trees), eggs (that we get to take from under the chickens), goats, of course (that we get to milk, just like cows), and some other stuff I can't remember. Pretty cool, huh?

Part of the reason why I'm extra excited about going to a farm is that I'm a foodie. Don't worry, a foodie isn't a weird sickness—it's a person who likes trying new foods! One of my best friends, Camille, is the reason

I became a foodie. She's from France, and in France they don't eat things like macaroni and

cheese and chicken nuggets for lunch. They eat salads with buttery lettuce, tiny beans, and cheese from goats. They even eat ducks. I ate a duck at Camille's house once and I actually liked it.

There are also some other lucky and exciting things happening, so I decided to make a list about them. I love making lists—in fact, I'm an expert at it. Even Mrs. B says so. Here's my list:

1. At Goat Hill Farm, we are also going to make a whole lunch out of the eggs, goat milk,

and apples without even going to the grocery store, and we get to eat it right there at the farm. It'll be like a big party!

2. I now officially have two best friends. I used to have only one best friend, Sage. Then Camille moved here and we became best friends, too.

3. Since Sage and Camille are both in my class, they'll go to the farm with me, which makes them pretty lucky, too.
4. We get to watch a movie today in class, which we hardly ever do. I just wish we could have popcorn to go with it.
5. Yesterday at Camille's house, for dinner, Mrs. Durand made fried artichokes, which is now my new favorite vegetable. An artichoke

is a very weird name for a vegetable, but I love it anyway.

The movie Mrs. B showed us was about how things grow. We watched a girl plant an apple seed with her mom. After they watered it, the seed grew into a little sprout. Then it grew into a big plant, and suddenly the girl was picking an apple off the tree and eating it. It was pretty amazing, but I think it might take a little longer in real life.

The coolest part of the movie was at the end, when the girl put the

apples in a pot with sugar and water and cooked them. They got all mushy and turned into applesauce. I didn't know you had to cook apples to make applesauce! I thought you just mashed them up a lot. But I did know that one thing was missing.

"Mrs. B?" I said after the movie.

"Yes, Phoebe?"

"We should bring some cinnamon to the farm." I heard Sage start to laugh. I gave him my best warning face, where I squint my eyes like a mean cowboy.

"Why's that, Phoebe?" Mrs. B said.

"Because I once heard Camille's

dad say that cinnamon and apples were meant to be together. Isn't that romantic?" I said. Camille's face started to turn the color of a bright red apple. Her face is always turning crazy colors like that.

Mrs. B smiled. "Huh, I've never

thought about it that way. But you don't have to bring any. The farm has a big kitchen, so I'm sure they have their own cinnamon."

"Oh, that's okay, I'll just bring a tiny little bit for emergencies," I said, pinching my thumb and pointer finger together to show Mrs. B just how little I meant.

Mrs. B sat down at her desk and rubbed her eyes.

Poor Mrs. B. Sometimes she seemed tired.

The night before my field trip, I gave my mom the list of what we needed to bring to the farm:

1. Hand sanitizer
2. A change of clothes
3. Water

I had also added a few things:

4. A small amount of emergency cinnamon (for the apples)

5 My purple polka-dot raincoat in case it rains (Grandma Green gave it to me for my birthday last spring. It's very shiny and the polka dots even have glitter on them, which makes it the most perfect raincoat ever.)

6 Matching boots (Who wears a raincoat without matching boots?)

7. My lucky watering can (It has my name stenciled on it, and everyone knows that things with your name on them are luckier than things without your name.)

"Pheebs," my mom said, sitting on my bed and staring at the list, "are you sure this is the correct list?"

I nodded.

"Part of it is typed and part of it is handwritten, in your handwriting."

"I had to add some extremely important things," I replied with a sigh. Sometimes Mom takes a while to understand things.

"So you felt that *emergency* cinnamon, whatever that may be, your raincoat, boots, and a stenciled watering can were extremely important?"

"Yes, absolutely," I said, getting my boots out of the closet.

"Uh-huh." Mom pushed her glasses up her nose. "Well, you can bring your boots. But not the raincoat and watering can. It's not even supposed to rain."

"Okay," I mumbled. When Mom uses her super-serious, super-calm voice, there's no use in arguing. Sometimes grown-ups don't get the big picture, you know? But Mom didn't say I couldn't bring the cinnamon.

GOAT·HILL
FARM

Chapter Two

When I woke up on Monday, I fed my blue betta fish, Betty #2, named after my first fish, Betty #1, may she rest in peace. Then I put on jeans, my apple shirt, and my purple polka-dot rain boots. I also found my floppy white beach hat, because

farmers in books usually wear straw hats, and my beach hat is almost like that. After I put on the hat, I thought I looked like a pretty great farmer.

I went downstairs early before anyone was in the kitchen and found a bottle of cinnamon. I dumped some in a baggie and stuck it in my pocket just in case. Then Mom came down and made me a big bowl of oatmeal my favorite way, with bananas, walnuts, and maple syrup, so I'd have some extra farm energy to do lots of farmy things.

"Have a great day at the farm," Dad said after breakfast, squeezing my shoulder.

“Bring me back an apple,” my big sister, Molly, called as she was putting things in her backpack.

“Oh, apples would be nice,” Mom said.

“I’ll try, but I can’t promise anything.” That’s what Dad always says when I ask him to bring me back

black-and-white cookies from the city. I patted the emergency cinnamon in my jeans, adjusted my floppy farm hat, and slipped on my backpack. Watch out, farm, here I come!

"Can I sit with you, Phoebe?" Camille asked me as we were going out to the buses.

"Okay," I said.

"Hey, I thought you were sitting with me!" Sage piped up from behind me.

I froze. I hadn't thought about riding on the bus with two best friends. Usually, Sage and I sat together, but I didn't want to say no to Camille.

"How about we all sit together?" I suggested, even though I knew we would be crowded. They looked at each other and nodded.

When we got on the bus, I found a seat in the back and we sat down, me in the middle feeling hot and squished.

"Hey, can you guys move over?" I asked.

Camille moved over a little bit. "I'm going to fall off if I move any more."

"Sage, can you?" I asked, fanning myself.

“Not unless you want me to jump out the window,” he said.

I slumped down in my seat. Maybe it wasn’t so lucky having two best friends.

After a hot and bumpy ride, we got to Goat Hill Farm. I expected to see goats running around everywhere, but

I didn't see any. The whole class got off the bus and lined up. We followed Mrs. B and the parent chaperones to the front of a building where a farmer lady was going to meet us. She wasn't wearing overalls or holding a pitchfork (I once saw a picture of farmers who looked like that), but she did have on a big straw hat, so she probably was a real farmer. She said her name was Jenna, and she told us three very important farm rules. This is what they were:

1. no touching or feeding the animals unless she said we could. (Easy.)

GOAT·HILL
FARM

2. We had to wash our hands before eating anything. (Kind of easy.)
3. We had to stay with the group at all times. (Super easy!)

"Now that we have the rules down, are we ready for some fun?" Jenna called out.

"Yeah!" I yelled back as loud as I could, but apparently nobody else was ready to have fun, because not a single other person answered. My cheeks started to turn red just like Camille's.

"Okay, who would like to try gathering some eggs?" Jenna asked when we got to the chicken coop. I glanced around me as I stepped into a dark place filled with chickens. They didn't seem scared of us, but I was a little scared of them. Jenna explained that chickens hatched eggs all day long, and that you had to put your hand under them to collect one.

"Phoebe, would you like to try?" Mrs. B asked. I spied some comfortable-looking chickens nesting in little wooden shelves over on the other side of the coop. The shelves looked like bunk beds.

"Okay," I said, but stood right where I was. I wasn't sure I wanted to put my hand near a chicken's egg-coming-out area.

"Why don't you stand over here?" Jenna said, pointing to the chicken bunk beds.

I slowly walked over and stared at one of the chickens. She stared right back at me with her funny little eyes. She almost looked like she was smiling.

"This is Elizabeth," Jenna said. "She's one of our best producers. She

wouldn't hurt a fly. Don't worry, just reach right in there." Jenna showed me how to slip my hand under the chicken and grab an egg.

I gave Elizabeth one last look in her tiny chicken eyes, held my breath, and stuck my hand under her. Then I felt it. A real live egg, all smooth and warm! I took it out. It was big and kind of bluish brown instead of bright white, which is what eggs usually look like at the grocery store. I held it up and felt just like I did when I won a soccer trophy last year. Pretty cool, huh?

"I got a real egg!" I called out. But as I held up my wonderful egg,

I didn't realize how delicate it was. I felt the shell collapse under my

fingers, and gooey yolk poured down my arm.

"Oops," Jenna said, smiling. "Let me get you a towel."

Sage doubled over laughing, and I have to admit it would have been pretty funny if it wasn't my egg and my arm. I glanced over at Camille, who had a very worried, slightly pink look on her face.

"Don't worry, Camille," I said as Jenna rubbed my arm all over with a damp towel. "It doesn't feel as gross as it looks."

Then it was Sage's turn. Jenna brought him over to another chicken, but that chicken didn't seem too happy, because this happened:

1. The chicken pecked at Sage's arm.
2. Sage said, "Hey!"
3. Apparently chickens don't understand what "Hey!" means, so she pecked him harder.
4. Sage yelped and fell backward.

"Sorry about that! These chickens can be unpredictable," Jenna said, helping Sage up. Sage gave me a

sideways glance and I tried not to smile, but the harder I tried, the harder I wanted to smile. Then I laughed out loud before putting my not-eggy hand over my mouth, and Camille giggled. Sage stomped over to us.

"Thanks a lot," he said, rubbing his

arm and using his extra-low serious voice, but he didn't fool me at all, because a smile sneaked onto his face anyway.

Chapter Three

When we finished collecting eggs and washed up, we headed to the goat barn. I couldn't wait to finally meet the goats! Inside the dark, hay-covered barn there was a big goat and four little ones jumping around a small shed in the middle. A ramp led up to its roof, and one of the babies was climbing up. It was really stinky, and lots of the kids held their noses.

“This is Ginger,” Jenna said, giving the mama goat a little scratch under her chin. “Goat milking can be a little

tricky, so you guys are just going to watch me do it. And later we're going to make cheese out of the milk," she said.

I jumped up with my hand in the air. Jenna pointed to me. "Wait, do you mean goat cheese?" I asked. Ever since Camille moved here from France and let me taste goat cheese at lunch, it's been my favorite thing in the entire world.

"The very one," Jenna said and smiled.

"It's like a dream come true," I whispered softly.

Then Jenna took her straw hat off,

brought Ginger to a little stand, and hooked a small box of something that looked like cereal onto the stand. Ginger put her head through a hole in the stand and ate her goat cereal. Jenna sat on a little stool and pulled at Ginger's sticking-out parts under her belly that were called udders,

and milk started to fill up the bucket underneath. I wondered how in the world we were going to make cheese out of that. The goat babies ran around in little circles, climbing up and down the ramp to the little shed over and over.

"Oh, they're so cute," Camille said,

clasping her hands together.

"I know!" I said. I didn't even know goats could be cute.

"I want one," Camille said.

"Camille, your parents won't even let you have a fish," I replied.

Camille looked down. "Maybe if I was extra good, they'd let me."

"You're always good," I said. "But you still don't even have a fish." I patted her on the back to make her feel better.

After Jenna milked Ginger,

we each got a paper bag with our name on it. Then Jenna led us up to the apple orchard. An orchard, Farmer Jenna said, is a field of fruit trees. I got to the top of the hill and looked around. Jenna was wrong. The orchard was more like a huge green *ocean* of fruit trees. Red apples hung on the branches like shiny round jewelry. Everyone in my class ran around grabbing as many apples as they could. After I picked a bunch, I bit into one. It tasted like the sweetest, crunchiest, most apple-flavored apple I had ever eaten.

Then we got to see where the

Camille
PHOEBE
sage

spinach and lettuce grew. Jenna pointed to green leafy bunches sticking out of the ground in rows, which we were going to pick for our lunch.

I raised my hand.

"Yes, Phoebe," Jenna said. I was surprised she knew my name.

"Do you have any buttery lettuce here? Camille brings salads with buttery lettuce for lunch all the time. It's very good." Camille, who was looking at the lettuce plants, suddenly stared at me with big nervous eyes. I knew she got a little embarrassed when I talked about her food in front

of people, but sometimes I couldn't help myself.

"Do you mean butter lettuce? Not in this crop. We just have regular old romaine," she said with a grin. "But I'll keep that in mind."

Then Mrs. B said we were going to go back to the main building to make lunch. It was kind of amazing that we didn't even need to go to the grocery store at all. This was what we were going to do:

1. Make goat cheese out of the goat milk, which sounded like an amazing magic trick to me.

2. Make omelets with the magic goat cheese, fresh eggs, and fresh spinach.

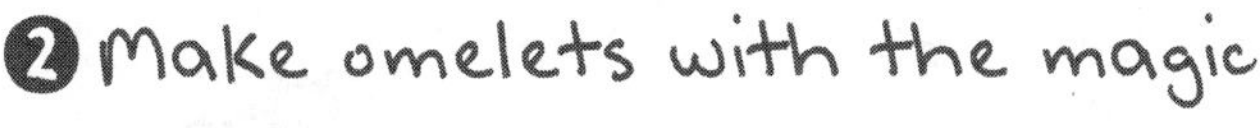

3. Make a big salad with all that lettuce,

because what else would you do with lettuce?

4. Make applesauce out of the apples for dessert.

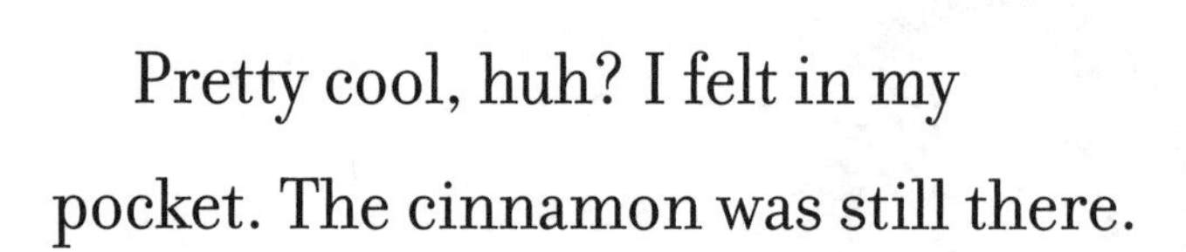

Pretty cool, huh? I felt in my pocket. The cinnamon was still there.

We headed down the hill and saw the goats again. Sage and I stopped to say hi to Ginger and her babies. Even after all that goat cereal, Ginger was chewing on the shed. The babies were doing the same thing. Could they still

be hungry? *Poor goats*, I thought, *stuck in this barn.* Maybe they needed a little exercise and fresh air.

Camille looked back at us. “Come on, you guys. Everybody’s ahead!” she said, so we rushed toward the farm kitchen.

When we got there, I stopped and

looked around. It was a big room with long tables and chairs in the middle and three different cooking places set up on the sides. Jenna stood at a counter with bowls of the lettuce and spinach we picked. Another farmer lady stood at a stove with the bucket of goat milk. A farmer man peeled apples at another stove.

"It's like a big cooking party!" I said, grinning from ear to ear.

"It looks like a lot of work to me," Sage said, his eyes wandering over the room.

I sighed loudly because sometimes I just have to sigh at Sage.

"Phoebe, don't make sighs at me," Sage said and crossed his arms.

"I wasn't," I said. "I was just catching up on my breath."

"Let's get in line," Camille said, and walked over to where Mrs. B and the parents were dividing people into groups. We followed.

"Don't worry," Mrs. B said. "Everyone will get to do everything."

Sometimes Mrs. B can read my mind.

Camille pulled me toward the salad group, but Sage wanted me to come to the applesauce group. I wanted to try the goat cheese first.

"Guys, I only have two hands," I said, because my mom says that a lot to me and Molly. Sometimes when you have two best friends, you have to be firm.

We all decided to try different things first. I went in the goat-cheese group. First we put lemon juice in the goat milk while it was cooking on the stove and it became bumpy, kind of like weird, watery oatmeal. Then we poured all that weird, bumpy goat milk into some bowls, each with cloth covering the

bottom and the sides. After we finished pouring, the farmer lady tied up the cloth pouches and hung them on hooks. Then all the liquid dripped out and the cheesy part stayed in.

"It really is a magic trick," I said. Mrs. B gave me one of her special winks.

Then Camille ended up in the applesauce group with me.

We chopped the apples into tiny pieces and put them in a pot with some water and sugar, just like in the movie we saw in school. The apples smelled good, but I knew something was missing.

"Excuse me," I said to the farmer man, raising my hand.

"Yes?" he said. He did not have a hat on, but he did have overalls, which looked sort of farmer-ish.

I coughed a little to make my voice very smooth and polite. "My friend's dad who is a chef of desserts from France says that apples and cinnamon are meant to be together, which is very romantic. Do you happen to have any growing on the farm? Like maybe a cinnamon orchard somewhere?"

The farmer man looked up and blinked. Then he laughed.

"No, we can't grow cinnamon here. It's too cold, but that's a nice idea. I think we might have some in this closet," he said, opening it and rummaging through. I felt for the cinnamon I had in my pocket, just in case.

"I think we're out of luck," he said after a minute. "Sorry about that."

"That's okay. I brought some for emergencies!" I said, pulling out the baggie and showing it to him. Camille's eyes looked like they were going to pop out of her head. Mrs. B was watching in the back.

"Well, aren't you prepared," the farmer man said, and after he took a sniff of my cinnamon, he let me sprinkle some in the pot. The smell changed from good to extra wonderful.

"Oh my, Phoebe," Mrs. B said, coming up to me and looking in the pot.

"I should have expected you might have something for us up your sleeve. Or rather, in your pocket!" she said, smiling.

After a long time, the applesauce was done, and all the water dripped out of the cheese pouches, leaving little balls of magical goat cheese. The salad was made, too, and the whole room smelled like cinnamon. We finally got to make the goat cheese and spinach omelets in a little pan. We mixed the eggs with spinach, salt, and pepper. Then we spread a little goat cheese on at the end while it was cooking. Jenna even knew how to flip the eggs over in the pan and fold them in half. After we cooked enough omelets for everyone, we set the table with paper plates, and each person got some omelet, salad, and a dish of applesauce.

"Wow," Jenna said to all of us, sitting at the head of the table.

She had taken her hat off and just looked like a regular person. "I've never seen a harder-working bunch of farmers! This is what we call farm-to-table eating, but I just like to call it farm fresh fun! We harvested our apples, spinach, and lettuce. We collected our eggs and milk. Then we made it into a wonderful meal. Now you see all the work that goes into just one lunch."

I took a bite of omelet. The warm goat cheese melted in my mouth. Then I had a forkful of crunchy salad and a spoonful of the sweet, cinnamony applesauce. The tasty buds on my tongue were about to explode in a happy way.

"Sage, isn't this the best cooking party you've ever been to?"

"It's pretty good," Sage said. "But I think it's much easier to buy hot dogs at the grocery store."

Camille and I just shook our heads at him. "Sage, I might have to sigh at you," I said. He shrugged, but then I didn't even sigh, because the taste of more goat-cheese omelet distracted me.

Chapter Four

After lunch, we were going to look at the greenhouse that wasn't green to see the way farmers are able to grow things even in the winter. Then, we would go back home on the bus. As we walked down the hill with our bags of apples to take home, I saw Ginger and her baby goats again. Ginger started *baaaa*-ing really loud. Then the cute babies did the same.

"What's wrong, little goaty goats?" I asked. Ginger started chewing on the gate lock. The babies copied whatever she did. Sage stopped with me, and we watched them for a minute while the rest of the class went on ahead.

"Maybe they need some exercise," Sage said.

"Well, what can we do?" I said and watched the goats paw at the gate.

"We could let them out for a minute. They could walk around a little and then go back in. No one will even notice."

"What if they run off?" I asked, wondering how easy the latch was to open. I lifted it up just to see, and before I knew it, Ginger had pushed her way out.

"Oh no!" I screamed as she practically ran me over, with the babies trotting quickly behind. Suddenly all five goats were running up the hill.

"Look!" Sage said. "They're going toward the chicken coop!"

We were about to run after them to try to chase them back in when Mrs. B

came down the hill, calling us.

"Phoebe, Sage, you need to stay with the group," she said.

"The goats got out!" Sage blurted. I just nodded very fast.

"What?" Mrs. B seemed very surprised. "How did they get out?" she asked slowly.

Sage shrugged, which is what Sage does when he doesn't know what to say.

"Phoebe?" she asked.

"Um, well, they pushed through the gate?" I said, feeling my face get very hot.

"How did they push through the

gate? Did you help them?"

Sage shrugged again.

"I don't know?" I said. For some reason, everything I said came out as a question. "They kept *baaaa*-ing and chewing on the gate and—"

"Okay," Mrs. B said. "We'll talk more about this, but we need to go tell Jenna right away."

Sage and I stood there nodding. I glanced up the hill and could see Ginger and the babies walking far away.

"*Now*, guys!" she said sternly, and I swallowed hard. We followed her over to the greenhouse.

"Jenna," Mrs. B said as we walked into the not-green greenhouse. "I'm so sorry, but Sage and Phoebe told me the goats got out of the barn. I think they have more to say, but I figured you'd want to see about the goats first."

Jenna's mouth opened and closed. Then she whipped out her phone.

"Tim, the goats from barn two are free. I think a couple of kids let them out."

Sage and I glanced at each other. "We just . . . ," Sage

started, but Mrs. B put her finger on her lips.

"We'll talk about it later," she said. "Just stay right here with the group."

All that yummy food I ate started to feel like a big heavy blob in my stomach, and I thought maybe Sage and I had made a big mistake.

Camille came up to me. "Did Mrs. B say you and Sage let the goats out?"

"Um, well, they sort of escaped," I said.

Mrs. B came over. "Phoebe and Sage, it looks like Jenna wants to talk to both of you now," she told us.

Uh-oh.

Chapter Five

Sage and I sat in Jenna's office with Mrs. B. I didn't know farmers even had offices. The parent chaperones had stayed with the rest of the class while they toured the greenhouse.

"The goats are wandering around the houses across the street. We've got a guy stopping traffic and a farmer with our sheepdogs out there trying to get them back," Jenna said, staring at us.

"Are they going to be okay?" I asked, thinking of the babies crossing the road. This wasn't feeling like farm fresh fun anymore.

She kept looking at us. "I laid out the rules pretty clearly. Why on earth

did you let them out?"

Sage and I sat quietly for a few seconds. Then Sage shrugged. He turned to me and shrugged once again. I was getting mad at Sage. He ruined the best farm trip ever! If he didn't want to talk, then I would.

"Sage said we should do it." I spoke in a squeaky voice.

Sage's mouth dropped open. "You opened the lock!"

"I did not!" I yelled. "Or at least I didn't mean to," I said more quietly.

"Well, guys, I wasn't there, so I don't know whose fault it was, but I do know those goats can't get out unless someone lifts the latch."

The tears started to make my eyes blurry. I rubbed my face a few times to chase them away. I looked at Sage. He stared at his boots with his arms crossed. His bottom lip trembled.

"I just played with the latch. I didn't know they would push through like that," I said.

"I understand how accidents can

happen, but I expected better behavior from you," Mrs. B said.

"You need to apologize to Jenna."

We both croaked out, "I'm sorry."

"Apology accepted," Farmer Jenna said as she stood up and nodded back at us, but she didn't smile. Then she gestured toward the door.

When we got outside, Sage yelled, "Look!" and pointed up the hill. I could see the goats running toward the barn. A black-and-white border collie ran after them, with the farmer man following behind. We all stood and watched.

"Go, goats, go!" Sage cried, jumping up and down.

They scattered a bit, and the mama

goat started making a turn toward a different field up ahead. The babies followed.

"Now they're heading the other way!" I exclaimed. My heart pounded through my shirt. Then another sheepdog came barking down the hill, nipped at the goats' heels, and chased them right inside the barn. The farmer quickly locked the gate after them.

"Thank goodness!" Mrs. B said.

I let out my breath and wanted to hug Sage. But when I looked at him, he looked away.

Mrs. B turned to Jenna. "Again, I'm so sorry about this. Sage and Phoebe

are good kids. I'm not really sure what got into them."

I'm not sure what got into us, either.

"Well, it's not the first adventure we've had on this farm," Farmer Jenna said as she straightened her big floppy hat and smiled a little. Then she looked serious again. "But one we could have done without."

Mrs. B led us back to the bus. I saw

everyone carrying their bags of apples.

I gulped. My apples! I must have lost them during the goat incident. Not only would Mom and Dad be mad at me, but I wouldn't have any apples to give them.

Back on the bus, I sat next to Camille. Sage sat with his friend Will.

I told Camille the whole story, and she listened extra carefully.

"Are you okay?" Camille asked when I finished, in her soft French way that made everything seem better.

"No," I said. "But I think I'll feel better someday. Maybe when I'm, like, thirty-two."

"I think you'll feel better at least by the time you're sixteen," she said, and put her long French arm around me. Then she pulled some things out of her pockets and handed them to me.

Apples!

"I took too many, anyway," she said.

“Oh, Camille. You’re the best French friend I’ve ever had!” I said. That’s another great thing about having two best friends. If one is mad at you for a ridiculous reason, and you are mad at him for a good reason, you can be with your other friend and not feel so mad.

When I got home, Mom was waiting for me at the door. She had her

trying-not-to-be-too-angry face on, where she scrunches her eyebrows together and bites her lip.

"Hi, Phoebe. I spoke to Mrs. B," she said as I walked in the door.

I dropped my backpack on the floor.

"She told me that you and Sage *might have* let some goats out?"

"I think so," I said, kicking my boots off.

"You mean you don't know if you did?" she asked, squinting at me.

I shook my head. I was all out of energy to explain it. "Only the goats know the truth," I whispered.

Mom stared at me for a second and put her hands on her hips. "Mrs. B is not too happy about this. I think you need to go to your room and think very hard about what happened. When Dad comes home, hopefully you'll remember the details."

Mom is always sending me to my room when she thinks I did something bad, but I actually didn't mind this time. I just wanted to lie on my bed and stare at the ceiling. Who knew farms were so exhausting?

Chapter Six

As I lay on my bed, I wrote a list of facts about the trip so I wouldn't forget. In not much time, Dad called me down for dinner.

He had made his famous spaghetti, which used to be called regular spaghetti and tomato sauce, but we made up a recipe where we added black olives, broccoli, and feta cheese, and then it became famous. When we sat down to eat, I showed Mom and Dad my list.

FIVE TRUE FACTS ABOUT HOW THE GOATS GOT OUT

1. Their barn was smelly and they needed more exercise.
2. They kept baaaa-ing and

chewing at the gate, which made me feel bad for them.

3. Sage felt bad for them, too.
4. Sage was the one who said that we should let them out, so it's really his fault.
5. I might have lifted the latch on the gate, and they might have pushed their way through, but if you want to know exactly what happened, you'll have to talk to the goats.

I handed the note to my dad, who read it and showed it to Mom.

"Pheebs," Dad started.

I looked at him.

"I'm glad you cared about the goats. But the farm has rules for a reason, and goats don't mind smelly barns the way you and I might."

"It really was an accident. I just touched the latch, and then they

pushed their way through. It was actually Ginger's fault."

"Who's Ginger?" Dad said.

"The mama goat."

Mom took a deep breath. "Well, next time you're at a farm and you're worried about an animal, tell the farmer. It's their farm, their animals, their rules. Got it?"

"Got it," I said quietly.

"And just because Sage says you should do something, it doesn't mean you should. If Sage told you to jump off a bridge, would you?" Mom asked.

I thought about it. I remembered a camping trip we took with Sage's family, and there was a little bridge over a creek. Sage said, "Let's jump!" And we did. But our parents said it was okay.

"How high is the bridge?" I asked.

"That's not the point!" Dad said.

"You promise never to do anything like that again," Mom said. "Right?"

"Right." I nodded.

"And no TV or computer time for a week," she said.

I knew that one was coming.

I nodded slowly. "Can I call Sage?" I asked.

"Now?" Mom asked.

I nodded. "I want to tell him that

if he asked me to jump off a bridge, I wouldn't do it."

Mom and Dad looked at each other and back at me.

"Okay," Mom said. "Right after dinner."

As soon as I finished eating, I dialed Sage's phone number. He answered right away, since we have our phone numbers on caller ID.

"Hi, Phoebe," he said.

"Sorry I tattled on you," I said very quickly, so I wouldn't not say it.

"Sorry I said we should let the goats out," he said with a funny sound

in his voice, like he was embarrassed.

"It's okay. Maybe that's why we're best friends. We're good in the same ways and bad in the same ways," I said.

"I never thought of it like that," he said, and we were quiet for a second or two.

"Sage?" I asked, making the quiet go away.

"Yeah?"

"Would you ever tell me to jump off a bridge?"

Sage was quiet again. Then he said, "How high is the bridge?"

I smiled. Even though I had to sigh at him sometimes, I smiled at him a lot more times.

After dinner, I saw Molly sitting at the kitchen bar, twirling on a stool, which was very strange. She was usually talking to her friends on the phone, doing her homework, or practicing her clarinet.

"How come you're just sitting there?" I asked. "Don't you have lots of thirteen-year-old stuff to do?"

She turned around. "Not really," she said and laughed.

"Oh," I said, and sat on the stool next to her, looking at my feet.

"Sorry about the farm trip," she said.

"It's okay," I replied. "You know what I'm most sad about, though?"

"What?" she asked.

"That I made Mrs. B upset," I said in a small voice.

Molly thought for a moment. She took another spin on the stool and stopped, facing me. "Maybe you could write a note to Mrs. B telling her how you feel, or make her something?"

I wondered what I could write or make for Mrs. B. Then I remembered I had my two apples from Camille.

"I know!" I said, pointing my finger in the air. "I'll make her an apple tart just like I had at Camille's!"

Molly smiled. "Maybe we could make one together," she said.

I jumped up and hugged her, knocking her off her stool, but she didn't even get mad. We called Mr. Durand for an apple tart recipe. He gave us one that he said "even elephants could make." I thought that was a weird thing to say, but I once heard that elephants were pretty smart, so I hoped it wasn't too hard. We rolled out the dough into a square, put the cut apples on it all nice and pretty, and covered it with melted butter, sugar, and lots of cinnamon, of course.

When it was done baking, I had to run out of the kitchen quick with my hands over my mouth so I wouldn't eat it.

The next morning, I carried my tart carefully wrapped in foil and saw Sage walking out of his house holding something in a jar.

"What's that?" I asked him when I caught up with him.

"It's apple chutney. I asked my mom if I could make something for Mrs. B."

"I made her something, too, see?" I said, uncovering my tart. "We *are* good in the same ways!"

"Wow," Sage said. "We just might be the baddest and goodest people we know!" We held our goodies carefully as we walked the rest of the way to school.

When we got into the classroom, we went right up to Mrs. B, who sat at her desk. The buses hadn't arrived yet, so only the kids who walked to school were in the classroom putting away their stuff.

"My sister and I made an apple tart from the farm apples," I said. "You get to eat the whole thing!"

I held up the tart.

"And my mom and I made you apple chutney," Sage

chimed in, holding up his jar.

"Wow, that's so nice of you both," Mrs. B said. "I can't wait to taste all of this." She put the tart and the chutney on the side of her desk. I was kind of disappointed because I wanted to see her eat the tart and maybe ask me if I wanted some, too.

"What did I do to deserve these treats?" she asked, taking off her green glasses that she wore on a beaded chain around her neck.

"I was the one who did something bad. So I put all my sorry feelings into the tart," I said.

"Yeah," Sage said. "I did that,

too." He pointed to the chutney jar.

"Maybe we could mail some to Farmer Jenna," I suggested.

Mrs. B laughed. "I'm not sure this would mail all that well, but I will tell her that you wanted to. I know you didn't mean for it to happen. I just want to make sure you both know how important it is to follow the rules."

"We know," said Sage, looking down. I nodded.

"But now that you understand, let's try these lovely things," she said, and pulled off a little piece of tart for herself.

"Oh, Phoebe! That's delicious!" she said with her mouth full. Then she tasted a spoonful of the chutney. "Fantastic, Sage. I'm serving this at my next dinner party!"

That's another thing I love about Mrs. B. She has really good taste.

Later, in the cafeteria, Camille waved me over and patted the seat next to her. I sat down and looked at Camille's lunch laid out, with a small piece of bread on a napkin, a cup of blueberries, and a pretty-looking salad with very curly lettuce, apples, and thin slices of Parmesan cheese that looked like little pieces of paper.

Then I saw Sage glancing over at us, holding his tray. I sighed. There wasn't a seat open next to me. That's one of the worst things about having two best friends. Lunch always needed to be figured out. We tried to sit together, but sometimes it didn't work. I hoped Sage wasn't going to feel bad. He started to march right toward us. Then I looked at Camille, and she was waving him over.

"I saved a seat for you, Sage," she said to him, and patted the seat on the other side of her. I wanted to give her a big hug, but I didn't want to knock her off her chair, so I just clapped my hands.

Sage grinned and sat down. He had the school lunch—a piece of very brown meat loaf, mashed potatoes, and green beans that were more brown than green. I had some pesto pasta that I made

with my mom, and artichokes, my new favorite vegetable. Camille and I traded tastes like we usually do. The sweet apples, bitter lettuce, and salty cheese did a dance in my mouth. After we ate our lunches, right when I was wishing I had a piece of that tart I gave Mrs. B, Camille took out some lemon cake and gave us both a piece. Pretty cool, huh?

As we chomped on the sweet, spongy cake together and made lots of "*mmmm*" sounds, I finally figured out the best thing about having two best friends—it's having two best friends.

Veera Hiranandani is the author of *The Night Diary* (Kokila), which has received many accolades including the 2019 Newbery Honor Award. She is also the author of *The Whole Story of Half a Girl* (Yearling), which was named a Sydney Taylor Notable Book and a South Asia Book Award Highly Commended selection. She earned her MFA in fiction writing at Sarah Lawrence College. A former book editor at Simon & Schuster, she now teaches creative writing and is the proud mom of two foodies, who even like to eat their vegetables (most of the time).

Christine Almeda is a Filipino American freelance illustrator and character designer from New Jersey, mainly known for her work in children's books. She believes in the power of creativity and diverse storytelling, and that art can make life more beautiful.